Balamory

BBC

The Clown

RED FOX

THE CLOWN
A RED FOX BOOK 0 099 48046 8
First published in Great Britain by Red Fox,
an imprint of Random House Children's Books
By arrangement with the BBC

Red Fox edition published 2005

1 3 5 7 9 10 8 6 4 2

Text and illustrations © Red Fox 2005

BBC © BBC 1996

 © BBC 2002

The BBC logo is a registered trademark of the
British Broadcasting Corporation and is used under licence.

Red Fox Books are published by Random House Children's Books,
61–63 Uxbridge Road, London W5 5SA,
a division of The Random House Group Ltd,
in Australia by Random House Australia (Pty) Ltd,
20 Alfred Street, Milsons Point, Sydney, NSW 2061, Australia,
in New Zealand by Random House New Zealand Ltd,
18 Poland Road, Glenfield, Auckland 10, New Zealand,
and in South Africa by Random House (Pty) Ltd,
Endulini, 5A Jubilee Road, Parktown 2193, South Africa

THE RANDOM HOUSE GROUP Limited Reg. No. 954009
www.**kids**at**random**house.co.uk/balamory

Photographs taken by Nigel Robertson   Text by Alison Ritchie   Designed by Clair Stutton

A CIP catalogue record for this book is available from the British Library.

Printed in Italy

Oh, hi there, I'm Miss Hoolie. Don't I know you?
  Today in Balamory it's a work day, and everyone is busy going to work and school.

"Oh, look what I've found – a make-up box! This is just what Giggles the clown needs. He's coming to the Nursery today. Josie will be here soon – she loves clowns!"

Here she is now!

"Hi, Miss Hoolie! I'm so looking forward to the clown show," says Josie.

"There's just one problem, Josie. Giggles left all his clown stuff on the ferry! But I've just found this make-up. Could you do me a favour and drop it round to my house for him?"

"Sure thing, Miss Hoolie! Anything to help get the show on the road!"

Which colour house do you think Josie will be visiting next?

"That's right," said Josie. "It's the house where Miss Hoolie lives."

"Giggles? Where are you?" calls Josie. "Aargh! What was that?" she squeals, nearly jumping out of her skin.

Honk! Honk!

First the white make-up . . .

then two rosy cheeks . . .

colour round the eyes . . .

. . . a big smiley mouth and

A BIG RED NOSE!

"Perfect, Giggles! You look great! Come on, let's get you to the Nursery!" laughs Josie.

But poor Giggles still looks sad.

"Oh dear! What's the matter now?" asks Josie.

"Oh! You still need all your other clown things, don't you? So you can juggle . . . and ride your unicycle and squirt water! Don't worry, Giggles, leave it to me! I'll go and see Archie. He's bound to have something!" Josie races over to Archie's castle.

"Here you are! There's everything a clown could possibly need in here," Archie declares.

"Oh Archie, that's brilliant! Come on, let's take it to Giggles right now!"

"Here you are, Giggles!
Everything you need
for your show," Archie
announces proudly.
  Giggles shakes his head.
  Archie looks surprised.
"Something's missing?
What could that be?"

"Aha!" laughs Archie. "You need some custard pies! Oh dear, where are we going to find custard pies?"

"I know!" smiles Josie and dashes out of the door . . .

. . . to Pocket and Sweet's!

"What can I do for you, Josie?" Suzie asks.

"Well, Giggles the clown needs some custard pies!" explains Josie.

"You're in luck!" Suzie smiles. "I've got all sorts of pies. What flavour would he like? Rhubarb custard, cherry custard, blueberry and pumpkin custard?"

"I'll take the lot, please!" says Josie.

"The lot? I hope Giggles doesn't eat them all at once!"

"Oh, they're not for eating, Suzie, they're for throwing!"

"Did you hear that, Penny? My custard pies for throwing! Oh no no no! My pies are yummy – they're for eating, Josie, not throwing."

"Don't worry!" Penny tells Suzie. "I have an idea!"

"Now THIS is a real clown's custard pie!" smiles Penny.

"Perfect!" says Josie. "Now Giggles can do his show. I'd better get him over to the Nursery!"

Giggles puts on a fantastic show.
THREE CHEERS FOR GIGGLES THE CLOWN!

So, what was the story in Balamory today?

Well, Giggles the clown was coming to put on a show, but he left his bag of clown things on the ferry.

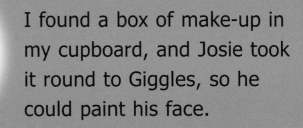

I found a box of make-up in my cupboard, and Josie took it round to Giggles, so he could paint his face.

He still needed all the rest of his clown things. Archie came to the rescue – he had juggling balls and squirty flowers . . .

. . . and Penny made the custard pies for throwing!

Giggles put on a brilliant show – it was SO funny!

So, that was the story in Balamory. Why don't you try clowning around some time? Bye!